BUGGED!

JANET LORIMER

PAGETURNERS®

SUSPENSE
Boneyard
The Cold, Cold Shoulder
The Girl Who Had Everything
Hamlet's Trap
Roses Red as Blood

ADVENTURE
A Horse Called Courage
Planet Doom
The Terrible Orchid Sky
Up Rattler Mountain
Who Has Seen the Beast?

MYSTERY
The Hunter
Once Upon a Crime
Whatever Happened to
  Megan Marie?
When Sleeping Dogs Awaken
Where's Dudley?

DETECTIVE
The Case of the Bad Seed
The Case of the Cursed Chalet
The Case of the Dead Duck
The Case of the Wanted Man
The Case of the Watery Grave

SCIENCE FICTION
Bugged!
Escape from Earth
Flashback
Murray's Nightmare
Under Siege

SPY
A Deadly Game
An Eye for an Eye
I Spy, e-Spy
Scavenger Hunt
Tuesday Raven

SADDLEBACK
EDUCATIONAL PUBLISHING
www.sdlback.com

ISBN-13: 978-1-68021-393-5
ISBN-10: 1-68021-393-8
eBook: 978-1-63078-794-3

Printed in Malaysia

21 20 19 18 17   1 2 3 4 5

PAGETURNERS® | SCIENCE FICTION

Chapter 1

Jean Wilson gazed in horror as the monster came closer. Its huge black eyes seemed to stare right at her. Sharp front claws reached out as if to grab her. A gaping mouth opened wide.

Jean sat on the couch. Next to her was her twin brother, Jared. He could hardly keep from laughing. The black-and-white movie Jean was watching had been made more than fifty years ago.

"Hard to believe Jean's in college," Jared teased. "Anyone can see that giant ant is a fake. Anyone but my sister, that is!"

Jared grabbed a couple pieces of popcorn. He tossed them at his sister. She didn't budge. "Man, you are so into it," Jared said.

He glanced at the clock. The baseball game was about to start. He didn't want to miss a minute of it. But first he had to pry Jean away from the old horror flick.

Jared reached out and poked his twin in the ribs. She jumped and screamed at the same time. This pleased him.

"Don't do that!" she yelled, glaring at her brother.

Jared laughed. "Oh, come on. You've seen that stupid movie a dozen times."

"Only three times," Jean said. "And it's a lot more exciting than a baseball game."

Now it was Jared's turn to glare. "Look, you promised," he said. "You said you'd turn off the movie when the game came on, remember? And I promised to go bug hunting with you tomorrow."

Jean sighed and stood up. "Oh, all right," she said. "But you'd better help me find some great specimens, or—"

"Or what?" Jared said, laughing. He

grabbed the remote and switched channels. "Don't think you can scare me by saying you'll put bugs in my sock drawer. Remember which one of us is studying insects."

Jean grinned. "I'm not threatening to put bugs in your socks. But how about if I show all the girls at school your baby picture?"

Jared picked up a pillow to throw at his sister. Then he noticed that the game had started. He threw the pillow down. "I'll get you later," he said.

Jean threw a handful of popcorn back at him. Then she wandered into the kitchen.

It was great to be home for the summer. She poured herself a glass of juice. With a happy sigh, she sat down at the kitchen table. She reached for the cookie jar.

Jean and Jared had grown up on Warm Springs Island. It was off the coast of Florida. The only way to get on and off the island was by ferry. On the west side was a harbor where the boats docked. A small business district was close to the harbor. Warm Springs was small. There was one main street and a handful of stores. A small hotel stood at one end of town. A supermarket was at the other.

During the summer, tourists came to the island to fish, camp, and swim. Some of the visitors had summer homes there. Most of the people who lived on Warm Springs all year long were fishermen and farmers. Jean and Jared's parents taught at the local high school.

When they were little, the twins had explored the whole island. They knew every inch of it. The beach had been their favorite playground. Climbing the old oak trees that grew there had brought them hours of fun. Even the limestone caves in the middle of the island had been a great place to explore.

After graduating from high school, the twins had moved to Miami. In college, they majored in science. Jared's field of interest was insects. Even as a small boy he had been fascinated by crawly things.

Jean shuddered. She remembered all the times her brother had played tricks on her with bugs. Jared had been the one who put bugs in her socks. What a shock it was when she opened her sock drawer!

"How's the game?"

Jean looked up. Her mother came into the kitchen. "Baseball's not my thing," Jean said. "And bugs aren't either. I was just thinking about tomorrow. I'm not looking forward to going out insect hunting."

"I thought school was out for the summer," her mom said. "Why do you have to go out looking for bugs?"

"Oh, it's just a favor I'm doing for one of my friends," Jean said. "She needs samples of different kinds of bugs from the island." She grinned. "Don't worry, I'm not going 'buggy' like Jared. Genetics is my real interest, Mom. You know I've always been curious about why people inherit certain traits. Like why we have brown hair and gray eyes. And why we're both so interested in science."

"Or why some people are musical and others are not?" her mother asked.

Jean nodded and bit into a cookie. "Of course, there's more to genetics than that. Like the fact that some families get certain diseases and other families don't. Knowledge of genetics is becoming more important to our health. And there are new discoveries every day." Then she smiled. "Collecting these bugs is just a good deed for a friend. She's taking a summer class."

Mrs. Wilson nodded and smiled. "You and Jared seem to have inherited a lot of curiosity, for sure."

Jean laughed. "Curiosity is a good trait for a scientist. And speaking of curiosity, what's going on with ..." Jean's voice trailed off. She stared at a huge, dark shadow crawling across the wall behind her mother. Oh my God! "Aahh!" she screamed.

Chapter 2

Mrs. Wilson quickly glanced over her shoulder. She gasped and then laughed. "Oh, Jean! You scared me half to death! It's just a bug crawling on the ceiling light. That's what's making the shadow."

Jean looked up at the ceiling fixture. Sure enough, a small beetle crawled on the glass. She slumped in her chair.

"I guess that stupid movie got to me after all," she said. "Now I'm seeing monster bugs! I'm going to have bad dreams tonight."

Jared came to the door. "I heard a scream. What's going on?" he asked.

Mrs. Wilson pointed at the ceiling light. "One of your friends came for a visit," she said with a grin.

The insect then dropped onto the kitchen table. It lay on its back. Its feet wriggled helplessly.

Jean made a face. "Ugh. Get that thing away from me," she said.

Jared laughed as he picked it up. "This little guy won't hurt you," he said. "Come on! Anyone can see it's just a harmless little beetle."

"I don't care what it is," Jean said. "It's ugly. And it has too many legs."

"Only six," Jared said. "Not eight, like a spider." He wriggled his fingers, imitating a spider's legs. Then he laughed at the expression on Jean's face.

"Hey, get a jar," he said. "Here's the first bug sample for your friend. That's one less bug to collect tomorrow."

The next morning Jean and Jared were up early. They packed a lunch. Then they put their equipment into the jeep. It was time to go.

"Have fun," their father said. "Oh, if you have time? Then drive by the park near the high school. Take a look at the town's latest effort to turn itself into a theme park."

Jean's eyes widened in surprise. "A theme park?" she asked.

"On a very small scale," her father said, chuckling. But he didn't really sound amused. "We won't be taking business away from Disney World or Universal. But we will have something new to draw tourists to the island."

Jared looked confused. "Are you kidding?" he asked.

"Don't you ever read my emails? No, he's not kidding," Mom said. "But it may not be as bad as your father says. Do you remember Rick Weaver? He's the one who came up with the idea to build it."

"I remember him," Jean said with a shudder. "That guy's creepy. When Rick Weaver smiles, he looks like an alligator."

"Hold on," Jared said. "Where did Weaver get the money? Seems like those big carnival rides would cost a lot."

"You're right," his dad said. "He probably borrowed the money from a bank on the mainland. If the park pulls in tourists as he hopes, he'll be rich." Mr. Wilson smirked. "He isn't doing this out of the kindness of his heart. I guess the park will provide summer jobs for a lot of the local kids, though."

"When will this amusement park get off the ground?" Jean asked.

"Tomorrow evening," her mom said. "Everyone in town is going to the grand opening."

"Hey, Jared," Jean said. "Maybe we should apply for a job. I could use the extra money. Even if it means working for Weaver."

Jared laughed. "Has anything else changed on the island?" he asked.

"As a matter of fact, yes," his father said. "You need to stay away from the old Lawson farm on the north shore."

Jared frowned. "Why? That place has been empty for years."

Mr. Wilson shook his head. "A group of people from the mainland bought the farm a few months ago. Word is that they don't like visitors."

"What are they doing out there?" Jean asked.

"No one knows," her father said. "But the new people aren't very friendly. Some folks say they've hired armed guards to patrol the place."

Jared whistled in surprise. "Thanks for the warning. We'll keep away."

The twins walked out to the jeep. Jean climbed in on the driver's side.

"Hey," Jared said. "How come you get to drive?"

"Because you have to look for bugs, remember?" she said with a grin. "After all, you're the expert!"

It was a perfect day for driving around the island. The sun beat down mercilessly. But a breeze kept everything cool. Mountains of big puffy clouds floated across the bright blue sky.

For the first hour or so, Jean followed the narrow roads that crisscrossed the middle of the island. Now and then Jared would tell her to pull over. Then they would both jump out of the jeep and start searching for bugs. By noon, they had collected several jars full of specimens.

"I'm hungry. Why don't we take a break for lunch?" Jean suggested.

"Good idea," Jared said. "How about if we have a picnic on the beach? Then we can go for a swim too."

"Sounds great," Jean said.

Jared climbed behind the wheel. "My turn to drive," he said.

Jean leaned back in the passenger seat. She looked around. "I had forgotten how pretty the island is," she said. "Remember when we were little? How we used to know every part of it?"

"Yeah," Jared said. "Remember the tree house we built in that big old oak?"

"I wonder if it's still there," Jean said.

"Let's go look," Jared said. He turned the jeep around. For the next few minutes the twins talked about all the good times they used to have playing in the old tree house. Then Jared slammed on the brakes. "Look!" he exclaimed. "There it is!" A huge oak tree loomed up beside the road. Yes! They could see the floor of the old tree house through the leafy branches near the top.

Jean laughed. "I don't believe it. The tree house is still here after all these years!"

She jumped out of the jeep. "I wonder if I remember how to climb this old tree."

"Just take it easy," Jared said. "The floor of the tree house may not—"

A loud boom drowned out his words. Jean screamed and dropped to the ground. Jared ducked. Then he climbed out of the jeep and crouched beside his sister. "Are you okay?"

She nodded. But her face was white with fear. "That was a gunshot," she said. "Someone is shooting at us!"

Chapter 3

A tall frowning stranger stepped from behind the oak tree. He carried a rifle. The barrel of the weapon was pointing down. But Jared had a feeling it could come up fast.

Jared's fear suddenly turned to anger. "What's wrong with you?" he yelled. "This isn't hunting season."

"I'm not hunting," the man said in a cold voice. "That was a warning shot. You two are trespassing."

"Huh? What are you talking about?" Jared said.

Jean grabbed her brother's arm. "Jared, look where we are. We weren't watching where we were going. We're pretty close to the Lawson farm."

"Private property," the man said. "Didn't you see the signs?" He pointed toward the trunk of the oak tree. Sure enough, a No Trespassing sign was sticking out of the ground.

Jared's burst of anger quickly turned to embarrassment. "I guess we didn't think to look," he said.

"Get back into your jeep. Turn around and get out of here," the man said. The barrel of the gun rose about an inch. Jared got the message.

Jean took out her phone. She was scared. But she didn't want to be intimidated.

"Come on," he said to Jean. "We'd better do what he says."

"Take all the pictures you want. *You* broke the law," the man said.

Jared's hands shook as he started the jeep and turned it around. He checked his rearview mirror. The scowling man with the gun stood in the road. He watched them drive away.

The twins didn't speak for a while. Then they got to a small cove on the east side of the island. This had always been a favorite spot for picnics. But today it seemed to have lost some of its charm.

Jean spread an old blanket on a flat stretch of warm sand.

Jared slumped against a rock. "Boy, that was a close call!" he exclaimed. "Dad was right when he said the new owners aren't friendly."

"The island was never like this when we were growing up," Jean said. She handed her brother a sandwich. "What do you suppose is going on at the Lawson farm?"

"I don't have a clue," Jared said. "But I intend to find out." He took out his phone.

Jean's eyes widened. "Oh no you don't," she said. "We could get into big trouble. That guy wasn't fooling around."

Jared shrugged. "Maybe Sheriff McKay knows what's going on. The question is why those people need armed guards. Are they doing something illegal? Dangerous?"

"Don't jump to conclusions," Jean said. "There may be a simple answer." She bit into her sandwich. "Still, we should report this to the sheriff. He needs to know that somebody could get hurt by those trigger-happy guards."

"Not just the locals either," Jared said. "What about the tourists? School is out now. We'll be getting lots of summer visitors. You know how tourists are. They go all over the island."

Jared searched his phone for information. But cell reception was poor. He didn't learn anything.

They finished eating. Then the twins headed back to town. The sheriff's office was about halfway down Main Street. Jared parked in front.

The twins walked into the sheriff's office. They heard angry voices coming from a back room. Sheriff McKay's deputy grinned at them. "Hey, you guys. Long time no see. How's school?"

"Great," Jared said. Then he frowned as the voices grew louder. "What's going on back there?"

The deputy smiled. "Do you remember Hannah Bowen?" he whispered. "She has a farm over on the north side."

"Yeah. Near the Lawson farm," Jean said. "I remember Hannah. Her husband died a few years ago. She's been trying to run the place by herself."

"Well, she claims the people who bought the Lawson place are a bunch of mad scientists. She thinks they're dangerous." The deputy shook his head. "That old lady's crazy!"

Jean and Jared looked at each other. "Maybe not," Jared said. "Today, we—"

At that moment Hannah Bowen stormed out of the back room. Sheriff McKay was right behind her.

"Now listen here, Hannah," he said. "Try to be reasonable. I can't arrest the newcomers with killing your cattle. You need to have proof."

"Come out to my place, Sheriff," Hannah yelled. "I'll show you what's left of the calf that was killed last night. I tell you, those people are up to no good!"

"Take it easy, Hannah. A wild dog probably got that calf," Sheriff McKay said. "You can't blame your neighbors just because you don't like them."

The elderly woman gave a snort of disgust. "What kind of neighbors take potshots at unknowing trespassers?" she asked. She glared at the sheriff.

"I didn't say they were nice people," McKay said. "But they did put up signs. And they did warn us—"

"I tell you they're doing something dangerous!" Hannah said. She slapped her hand down on the deputy's desk. The deputy jumped in surprise. Jared and Jean tried hard not to smile. Hannah was a real fireball when she got mad.

"Take it easy, Hannah," the sheriff said. "I'll come out and take a look this afternoon, okay? Meanwhile, you get that temper of yours under control."

Hannah glared at him. "You don't deserve to be sheriff!" she cried. Then she stormed out of the office. The door banged loudly behind her.

Sheriff McKay rolled his eyes. Then he noticed Jean and Jared. "Well, hello there," he said. "What can I do for you today?"

Jean nudged Jared. "Go ahead," she said. "Tell the sheriff what happened. I want to talk to Hannah."

Before Jared could answer, Jean was out the door. She could see Hannah at the end of the block. Jean ran down the sidewalk. She caught up with the older woman just as she opened the door of her battered pickup.

"Hannah, wait!" Jean called out. She tried to catch her breath. "I wanted to ask you something."

"Don't you call me crazy too, Jean Wilson," Hannah said.

"I don't think you're crazy," Jean said. Then she told Hannah about the armed guard she and Jared had run into.

Hannah listened, nodding now and then. "The same thing happened to me last night," Hannah said. "I had gone out looking for that calf. He'd gotten out of his pen. But when I found him ..." Hannah's eyes filled with tears.

Jean hugged her. "I'm so sorry," she said. "But I need you to tell me exactly how the calf died."

Hannah sniffed. Then she wiped her eyes. "When wild dogs kill, they tear the animal open. You can see how they pull the meat off the bones. The bite marks are clear. But the calf didn't look like that. All that was left was skin and bones. Everything else was gone."

Hannah looked hard at Jean. "Do you understand? Whatever ate the meat could only have gone in through the eyes. Or the mouth. Something ate that calf from the inside out!"

Jean gazed at her in horror and disbelief. "So when did you run into the armed guard?" Jean asked.

"I'd just found what was left of the calf," Hannah said. "Then this man suddenly marches out of the trees. He waves a gun at me. Tells me I'm trespassing. *Trespassing*! People on this island have never put up signs and shot at each other. What's going on here?"

"I don't know," Jean said. "But I sure would like to know what killed your calf. Other animals might be in danger too. Did you really tell the sheriff that the people at the Lawson farm are mad scientists?"

Hannah nodded. "I certainly did. And I can prove it too." She leaned closer and lowered her voice. "I found this in what was left of the calf."

She pulled a plastic bag out of her pocket. Inside was a strange-looking object about three inches long. It was brown and fairly smooth. It looked like a large pod of some kind.

"What is it?" Jean asked with a frown.

"I don't know," Hannah said. "I tried to show it to the sheriff. But he wasn't interested. He said it must be a seed. Ha! I sure don't know of any plant on the island with seeds this size."

"May I have it?" Jean asked. "Jared and I can take it to the lab at the high school."

The older woman's eyes narrowed. She pushed the bag back into her pocket. "Sorry, Jean. But I have other plans for this seed. Or whatever it is. I know a man in Miami who will be very interested in it."

Jean sighed. She could see Hannah's point. She and Jared were only students.

"Tell you what," Hannah said. "Come out to my place. Maybe we can find some more of these seeds."

Chapter 4

Jean met her brother at the jeep. She told
Jared what Hannah had said about the calf.
"I want to go there. See it for myself," she
said. "And I want to help Hannah look for
more of those strange seeds."

"Are you sure it's a seed?" Jared asked.

Jean shook her head. "I don't know.
What else could it be?" she said.

"But how could a seed hurt a calf?"
Jared asked.

Jean shrugged. "I don't know. Unless
it was poisonous. Maybe the calf ate it."
She stopped and thought about that for
a moment. "But Hannah said she'd never
seen anything like it on the island."

"Maybe not. But that still doesn't explain

what ate the calf," Jared said. "Okay, let's go talk to Hannah."

On the road leading out of town, Jared drove by the high school. A wire fence enclosed the park next door. The twins could see carnival rides being tested. Game booths were getting final coats of paint. There was a big sign over the front gate.

WARM SPRINGS
AMUSEMENT PARK
OPENING SOON!

A large trailer sat outside the gate. Small groups of teenagers were going in and coming out.

"That must be the hiring office. That's probably where we go to pick up job applications," Jean said. "Or do you think we do that online?"

Jared pulled over and parked across the street. He stared at his sister. "Are you serious about this? Do you really want to spend your summer running a Ferris wheel or something?"

"Why not? There aren't a lot of other jobs on the island," Jean said. "And it would be nice to have the extra cash."

Jared sighed. "Okay. Why don't we find out"—he stopped and stared—"Look at that, Jean."

A black limousine pulled up in front of the trailer. It had tinted windows. Two men wearing suits and dark glasses got out. Then Rick Weaver came out of the trailer with a big smile on his face. The three men greeted each other like they were old friends.

A moment later Sheriff McKay's patrol car pulled in behind the limousine. The sheriff got out of his car and joined the group.

"Can you see the license plate on that limo?" Jared asked. "It's one of those vanity plates."

"No, I can't see it from here," Jean said.

"It says *HybriGene*," said Jared. "Did you ever hear of a business on this island called HybriGene?"

Jean shook her head. "Do you suppose they're the people who bought the Lawson farm?"

Jared shrugged. "For unfriendly people, they sure seem to be friendly with the sheriff and Weaver."

Jean was quiet for a moment. "Maybe the sheriff already knows what's going on out at the farm," she said. "Maybe he knows but isn't telling."

"Huh. Maybe," Jared said. "But what does Weaver have to do with HybriGene?"

"Let's get out to Hannah's place while it's still light," Jean said.

Hannah's farmhouse had the same worn and battered look as her pickup. "This place could sure use a fresh coat of paint," Jared said.

"Poor Hannah. I'm sure she doesn't have a lot of money," Jean said.

Jean knocked on the front door. After a moment the door opened a crack. The old woman peered out.

"It's okay, Hannah," Jean said. "It's just me. I told you I'd be out later to see the calf and—"

"It's gone," Hannah said sharply.

Jean looked puzzled. "What?"

"They came and got it. Took it away. I guess I made a mistake, Jean. I was wrong to jump to conclusions. They aren't such bad folks after all."

Jean glanced at Jared as if looking for an answer. Her brother shook his head and moved down the porch to the front window. Jean saw him peek inside.

"What happened? Who took the calf away?" Jean asked. "Was it the people from the Lawson farm?"

"I was wrong. I'm sorry I bothered everyone," Hannah said. She started to close the door.

"Wait, Hannah!" Jean cried. "Do you still have that strange seed?"

She heard the woman gasp just as the door slammed shut.

For a moment Jean stared at the door. She couldn't believe it. Then she started to knock again. But Jared shook his head. He put his hand on her fist. "What?" she asked.

"Come on," he said.

Jean turned to follow him down the front steps. "Jared, wait!" she said. "We can't just leave. I'm worried about Hannah. She's out here alone and—"

Jared leaned closer. He lowered his voice. "When I looked in the window, guess what I saw on the table? A check from HybriGene. I couldn't quite make out the amount. But I saw a lot of zeroes. I'll bet that company paid for the calf to buy Hannah's silence! That means they must have been behind the death of the animal."

Jean looked disappointed. "Well, I can't really blame her," she said. "She can sure use the money."

Jean was quiet for a moment. And then she asked, "What about that seed?"

"If that seed thing is so important," Jared said. "There will be more of them. And there may be more dead animals too. Let's take a good look around this part of the island. The guards can't keep us off public land."

"It's too late to start today," Jean said. "But there's something else we can do. We can call some of the people who have farms nearby. Maybe some of them have lost animals too."

"Good idea," Jared said. "And I can make some calls to the mainland. I'll do some online research too. I want to track down HybriGene. Find out just what kind of company it is. There's something rotten going on here."

The twins climbed back into the jeep. On the way home neither one had much to say. Both seemed to be lost in thought.

Then all of a sudden Jared screamed in pain.

Chapter 5

Jean grabbed the steering wheel. Her brother twisted in agony. She could see that he was tugging at his hair. But she couldn't tell what was wrong.

She was finally able to pull on the hand brake. The jeep skidded to a sudden stop.

Jared slumped back into his seat. Then he dropped his hands. Jean saw that a patch of his hair was soaked with blood.

"What happened?" she gasped. Where was the first aid kit? She frantically reached under the seat for it.

"Something flew at me!" Jared said in a shaky voice. He opened his fist. A huge green-and-black striped insect lay crushed in the palm of his hand.

Jean gazed in horror at the giant bug. "What is it?" she cried.

Jared didn't seem to hear her. He was staring at the bug like he couldn't believe his eyes.

Jean shivered. First things first. She found an antiseptic wipe in the first aid kit. Then she began cleaning the wound.

Jared jerked away. "Ow! That hurts!"

"Hold still," she said. "This is nasty. What kind of bug is that?"

"One I've never seen on the island before," Jared said. "It looks a lot like a cockroach, but ..." He shook his head in disbelief. "But not like any cockroach I've ever seen or read about."

Jean frowned. "We have cockroaches on the island," she said. "I've seen Mom put out roach traps."

"Yeah," Jared said. "But not this species. Or whatever this is." He shrugged. "Still, there are about five thousand different cockroach species in the world. And roaches are everywhere! So maybe I just never noticed this one before."

"I never heard that cockroaches bit people," Jean said.

Jared looked puzzled. "What are you talking about?"

"I'm talking about this thing biting you," she said. "Look." She held up the antiseptic wipe. It was stained red.

Jared looked at his head in the rearview mirror. "I don't believe this!" he cried. "I thought it just scratched me when it flew into my hair."

"No way! You've got a nasty little hole in your head," Jean said. "Are cockroaches poisonous? Should we get you to a hospital?"

Jared shook his head. "No, but roaches are dirty. Now this guy ..." He studied the roach. "This one's about the same size as a sewer roach. Did you know those bugs can swim up to a mile underwater? That's how they get into people's houses. They swim up through the drainpipes."

Jean felt her stomach lurch. "No wonder I hate cockroaches."

"Most people do," Jared said. He gazed at the insect. "But cockroaches are really amazing, you know. They've been around for millions of years. They can survive under conditions that kill off most other animals."

"You sound like you actually admire the ugly things," Jean said.

"Nah, not really. I just admire the way they adapt," Jared said.

"Do you admire the way this one chewed a hole in your head?" Jean said. "Hold still while I get a bandage."

After dinner Jean went into her room. "I want to find out if anyone else has lost any cattle," she told Jared. "I'm going to make a few calls. Send some texts."

"Go ahead," Jared said. "I'm going

online to do some research. I'll email a couple of my professors too. They may be able to help me figure out exactly what kind of roach this is."

Later the twins compared notes. "I talked to most of the old-timers who farm out on the north shore," Jean said. "Nobody seems to have lost any animals."

"I haven't had a lot of luck either," Jared said. "I emailed the picture of the roach to a couple of guys I know in Miami. They said they've never seen anything like it. But I did get lucky with HybriGene."

"Oh yeah?" Jean looked up. Her eyes were bright with interest.

"HybriGene is a company that's doing research with genetics. Most of their research has to do with plants. You know, like producing new types of corn and rice that resist plant diseases. Genetically modified organisms. GMOs are big right now."

Jean nodded. "Yeah. People don't trust

GMOs. Who wants to eat a mutant GMO potato? Is that what HybriGene is doing? I can see why they'd want to keep people away. A company that produces those kinds of plants certainly has big secrets to protect."

"So we're back to the beginning," Jared said wearily. "Sounds like there's nothing much to worry about except the gun-happy guards."

"Don't forget about that strange seed," Jean said.

"Maybe HybriGene has created a weird plant that produces poisonous seeds." Jared sighed. "I guess maybe we'll never know. Unless you want to go exploring tomorrow."

A scream from their mother interrupted the conversation. The twins dashed to the kitchen.

"It's your father!" Mrs. Wilson cried. She stood frozen, pointing out the screen door. "Go out and help him!"

The twins ran to the door. Their father

was kneeling at the foot of the steps. It looked like he had fallen. Blood ran down his face. Jared started to push the door open. Jean yanked it shut. "What are you doing?" Jared yelled. "Dad's hurt! We've got to help him!"

"Look what's on the screen," Jean said. She pointed a shaking finger at the middle of the screen door.

The dark shape on the screen looked very much like a giant cockroach.

Chapter 6

The enormous rust-colored bug was close to five inches long. The twins could see its huge dark eyes very clearly. As they stood staring, the giant bug slowly spread its wings. Jean gasped in horror. Its wingspan was almost eight inches from wingtip to wingtip!

"I see it, but I don't believe it," Jared said softly. "Mom, have you got any bug spray?"

Mrs. Wilson was desperate to get to her husband. But she ran to the sink and brought back a can. "Will that be strong enough?" she asked.

"I just want to make that thing fall off the screen," Jared said. He started to spray the bug through the wire mesh. Almost at once, a loud hissing sound filled the air. "No!" Jared said in a worried voice. "This can't be!"

"What is it?" Jean cried.

The bug thrashed. Then it tumbled off the screen.

"I'll tell you later," he said. "Right now we have to go get Dad."

He grabbed one of his mother's frying pans. Then he opened the door carefully. The bug lay on its back. It was barely moving. But Jean could tell it was struggling to stay alive.

Jared reached out to put the pan over the roach. "Kill it!" Jean shrieked.

"Don't!" Jared yelled. But he was too late. Jean had already grabbed the pan. She smashed the roach. The air was instantly filled with a terrible smell.

Jean put her hand over her nose and mouth. "Oh, that's gross!" she groaned.

"Roaches are well-known for their bad smell," Jared said. Then he sighed. "Jean, why did you have to smash it? It would have died under the pan! There goes my fantastic specimen. I didn't even have time to take a picture."

"Oh, Jared, I'm sorry! I just thought—"

"Ha! You didn't think at all," he snapped. "Well, too late now."

The twins quickly helped their father to his feet. They led him into the house.

"What happened, Dad?" Jared asked.

"I was taking the garbage out," Mr. Wilson said. "Suddenly, something flew right at me. It grabbed onto my face. I tried to brush it off. But it held on and just kept biting me."

"I think we need to take you to the hospital," Mrs. Wilson said.

"I agree," Jean said. "Dad's wound is worse than yours, Jared."

Jean and Jared helped their father to his feet. The family headed to the garage.

"When you saw that bug, you seemed

really surprised. Why?" Jean asked Jared.

"There's a gigantic cockroach in South America. It gets big like that one," Jared said. "It can grow up to six inches long. The bug's wingspan is a foot."

Jean felt sick to her stomach. "Oh, that is so disgusting!"

"But when I sprayed the roach that attacked Dad," Jared went on. "It hissed at me. In Madagascar there's a roach that makes a hissing sound. In fact, some people there like to keep the hissing roaches as pets."

"That's gross!" Jean cried. "I can't imagine it."

"That's the point," Jared said. "I never heard of a roach that grows huge and hisses."

"What are you saying? Have we discovered a new species?"

Jared shrugged. "I don't know what we've found. I'm going to have to do some more research."

At the hospital the doctor checked the wound on their dad's head. It quickly became clear that he didn't believe the story the twins told him.

"Maybe it was a bat," the doctor said with a smile. "They fly around at night. Of course they don't really fly into people's hair. But if this one was sick or injured, maybe it lost its way."

"This was not a bat," Jean insisted. "I saw it. It was a bug."

"Sure," the doctor said. "Well, you said you killed it. If you didn't smash it too badly, bring it around to the lab. We'll let the experts decide."

The doctor was humoring her. Jean could tell.

After the wound was dressed, the family drove home. "Well," Jean said. "We've seen two huge meat-eating roaches in one day. They must be what killed Hannah's calf."

"You and Jared need to talk to the sheriff," her mother said. "Your dad and I will back up your story. Then Sheriff McKay will have to believe you."

"Oh, sure, like the doctor," Jean said in a sarcastic voice. "I could kick myself for smashing that roach. I hope we can go out tomorrow and find another—"

Then, without warning, Jean slammed on the brakes. The car fishtailed. Then it came to a lurching stop. "What is it?" Mrs. Wilson cried out.

"Look!" Jean said in alarm.

The jeep's headlights were shining on a dead animal. It was lying by the side of the road. From what they could see, the fallen creature looked like a deer. But in the dark it was hard to tell.

The animal's body seemed to be wriggling about in a weird, unnatural way. Then Jean realized what she was seeing. The body was filled with huge cockroaches! As the Wilsons watched in amazement, several of the giant bugs crawled out of the deer's mouth. Then they flew away.

Now Jean remembered something that Hannah had said. Her calf seemed to have been eaten from the inside out!

Mrs. Wilson made a gagging sound. She turned her head. "Oh, please, Jean. Drive on. I can't stand to look at it!"

"Wait a second," Jean said. "I should try to film—"

"No!" her parents both yelled at the same time.

"Have you lost your mind?" her father shouted angrily. "Do you want to end up like that dead deer?"

Jean sank back into her seat. "No," she said. "You're right. It's too dangerous."

"Let's call the sheriff," Mr. Wilson said. "Jared, you make the call."

But Sheriff McKay wasn't in his office.

"Aw, come on, Jared," the deputy said. "This isn't funny. The sheriff won't be at all amused with your story about big bugs."

"But it's true," Jared insisted. "You have to send someone out to Old Oak Road. It was about a mile from the hospital on the—"

"I'll leave a message for the sheriff," the deputy said in an unfriendly tone. "He'll get back to you in the morning." And with that he hung up.

Jared ended the call. "No one is going to believe us," he said. "The deputy thinks we're hysterical crazies. Or that we're trying to play a childish joke on McKay."

"We need to get our hands on a specimen," Jean said. "That's the only way we can prove we're telling the truth."

Chapter 7

Jared woke Jean at sunrise. "Come on," he said. "I want to get back to that deer. We need to collect some specimens."

Jean rubbed her eyes and sat up. "I had the worst night," she said. "I dreamed I was being chased by—"

"Don't say it," Jared interrupted her. "I had the same bad dreams myself. Come on, Jean. Rise and shine!"

An hour later, they were in the jeep. Jared was behind the wheel. "Some vacation this is turning out to be," Jean said as they drove toward town.

"Keep an eye out for that dead deer," Jared said. "You're the one who spotted it first. Are we getting close?"

"Jared, it was dark," Jean said. "We were about a mile from the hospital. I remember that the road curved. Oh, look! There's the deer. Or what's left of it."

Jared pulled to the side and parked. They crossed the road carefully. "Stay back," he said. "And get ready to run if one of those roaches flies at you."

All that was left of the dead deer was a pile of skin and bones. Jared picked up a branch and carefully poked at the remains. "No bugs. They seem to be gone," he said.

"All of them?" Jean asked in disbelief. "But the body was absolutely crawling with roaches last night."

"Roaches usually come out at night to eat," Jared said. "In daylight they find a safe place to hide."

"Where could they be hiding?" she asked. "This island is a big place."

"Good question. Here's a better question. Where did they come from to begin with?"

"What do we do now?" Jean asked. "We need actual proof. The sheriff will never believe us without it."

"I've been thinking about that," Jared said. "Remember how Hannah acted when you asked if she still had the seed? She didn't say no."

Jean frowned. "I thought you said that seed had nothing to do with the roaches," she said.

"Well, I don't think it was a seed," Jared said. "I'm pretty sure it was an egg case."

Jean gasped. "Ew! So you think these giant roaches are breeding?"

He nodded. "I'm afraid so. Come on now. Let's go talk to Hannah again. If I'm right, that egg case will be the proof we need."

They reached Hannah's place. But there was no sign of the old woman. "Her truck is gone," Jean said. "She probably went to town."

"Or maybe to the mainland," Jared said.

"Look at the animal pens over there. Her cattle are gone."

"So are the chickens and pigs," Jean said, looking around. "Maybe she sold off her animals and left for good. That was fast!"

"Well, that huge check I saw would certainly have given her a fresh start," Jared said. He ran up the porch steps and peered inside. "Yeah, it looks like Hannah took off."

Jean sighed. "Our bad luck. There goes our last hope for proof."

"Not necessarily," Jared said with a grin. He turned the knob on the front door. It wasn't locked.

"Jared! Isn't breaking and entering against the law?" Jean asked.

But Jared pushed the door open. He went into the house anyway. "We aren't breaking in," he said. "We're just entering. Come on."

The twins began to search the house. After a few minutes Jean was about to give up. Then she heard Jared let out an excited yell. "Look, Jean! I've got it!"

She hurried to the kitchen. "Where did you find it?" she asked, gazing at the plastic bag in her brother's hand.

"In the garbage can under the sink," Jared said. "And this baby is just what I thought it was. It's a roach egg case. But I've never seen one this big."

"So, what now?" Jean said.

"Now we go talk to the sheriff. McKay may be a small-town cop, but he's not stupid."

"Well, thank you for that at least, Jared Wilson," McKay's voice called out from the doorway.

The twins whirled around in surprise. "How long have you been standing there?" Jared asked.

"About ten seconds," McKay said. "Hannah's neighbors saw you guys go into the house. So they called me. I happened to be cruising in the area. I came over right away."

"Now look, Sheriff, I know you think our story about giant roaches is—"

"I believe you," McKay said. He took a closer look at the egg case and let out a low whistle. "I'm afraid we have a problem on our hands."

"No kidding," Jared said disgustedly. "You want to tell us what's going on?"

McKay nodded. "I think you guys had better come with me." He saw the doubting look that passed between the siblings. "It's not what you think. Yes, HybriGene is behind the problem. But they're doing everything they can to solve it. Remember, tonight is the night the amusement park opens."

"Sheriff, can't you just close down the park?" Jean asked. "If you don't, you'll have hundreds of people on the island. What if thousands of meat-eating roaches are out flying around?" She shuddered. "It could be a disaster!"

McKay frowned. "We know that," he said. "But I'm afraid it's too late now. People are already pouring into town. Let's get over to HybriGene. I want the scientists to hear your story."

The twins agreed to ride with the sheriff. They wanted to hear more about the super roaches.

"Right from the start, HybriGene told us their work was top secret," the sheriff said. "They said they had their own guards to patrol their land."

"Didn't you wonder what they were doing out there?" Jean said.

"I checked into the company," the sheriff said defensively. "The report said they were doing genetic research with plants. Definitely not animals."

"So they lied to you," Jared said.

The sheriff sighed. "Not really. They

never said what they were going to do on the island. I guess I just took it for granted that—"

"So what are they doing?" Jared interrupted.

"Well—" the sheriff began to say.

"I bet I can guess," Jean said, cutting him off. "They're designing super cockroaches. They're combining the DNA of different kinds of roaches to help them create one huge and horrible roach."

McKay looked surprised. "How did you figure it out?"

"Jared said he'd never seen a hissing roach of that size," Jean said. "But the ones we saw are worse than just big. They're meat eaters that attack people and animals."

The sheriff nodded. "That's the problem," he said. "Their project got out of hand."

"But why make a super roach to begin with?" Jean asked.

"That's easy," Jared said excitedly. "So

they could make a poison that would kill it. Roaches adapt very quickly to new poisons. So any one kind of poison is only good for a while."

"I see," Jean said. "The super roaches were going to be used as test subjects. And HybriGene would stand to make a fortune. That is, if the scientists came up with a poison that could wipe out all kinds of roaches quickly."

"Getting back to this super roach," Jared said. "I bet there was some kind of accident, wasn't there? Some of the bugs got out of the lab. Right, Sheriff?"

Chapter 8

Sheriff McKay sighed and nodded. "That's what happened," he said. "At first HybriGene tried to keep the accident a secret. They thought they could find all the bugs and kill them."

"How stupid!" Jared said. "They knew what could happen. This could be an ecological disaster! How long have the roaches been in the wild?"

The sheriff shook his head. "I'm not sure. A few days, I think. Maybe a week. By the way, I only found out about this after I talked to Hannah."

"That was yesterday," Jared said. "Jean and I saw you and Rick Weaver at the park.

We wondered if those people were from HybriGene."

McKay nodded. "Weaver wanted to keep the whole thing covered up. After all, HybriGene advanced him the money to build the amusement park. Weaver figured he could hardly say no."

Jean groaned. "I knew there was a good reason I didn't like that man!"

"I gave HybriGene twenty-four hours to find the bugs and kill them," McKay said. "I guess I was wrong to wait so long. This morning I've already had dozens of reports of dead animals."

"It won't be long before the reports are about dead people," Jared warned. He pointed to the bandage on his forehead.

McKay looked miserable. "I know. We only have a few hours to locate those bugs and destroy them."

Jean felt sick with dread. "Don't you

think we should try to get everyone off the island first?" she said.

"That would take too long," the sheriff said. "So would calling in the FBI. Do you think we can do this by ourselves? You two know this island as well as anyone. If you can think of where those bugs might be nesting."

They had reached the Lawson farm. An armed guard stopped the sheriff's car at the front gate. The man peered in at Jean and Jared. "Sorry, Sheriff, we can't have any outsiders—"

"Oh, knock it off!" the sheriff cried angrily. "You guys have a much bigger problem than your so-called security. Now let us through."

"Okay, okay," the guard said as he quickly opened the gate.

They reached the house. A gray-haired man in a white lab coat was waiting for them. "That man is Dr. Swanson," the sheriff said.

"He's the chief scientist who heads up the local product development team."

"Sheriff, how much time do we have before the amusement park opens?" Jean asked.

The sheriff glanced at his watch as they climbed out of the car. "About six hours," he said.

Jared frowned. "Jean, can you think of where those bugs might hide? I've got a couple of ideas, but—"

"We need to take a good look at a map of the island," Jean said.

"Come inside," Dr. Swanson told them. "We've got just what you need."

HybriGene had turned the Lawson farmhouse into its main office. A huge Google Earth map of Warm Springs Island was on a large computer screen. Jared gazed at it.

"I've been thinking about Hannah's barn," he said. "I didn't see any bugs in there. But what about some of the other farms? Barns are dark and warm."

"Good idea," the sheriff said. "I'll have some of my men start searching right away."

"Cellars and basements," Jean said. "What about houses that are empty right now? The homes of summer visitors?"

"Good," the sheriff said. "Trouble is, it's going to take hours to check out every possible summer home. I don't think we have that kind of time."

"How about getting some of the people who live on the island to help?" Jared suggested. "We can use social media to get the word out."

The sheriff shook his head. "Too dangerous. They may get hurt."

"I don't think we have any other choice," Jean said. "We're going to need all the help we can get."

♦ • ♦

The hours flew by. Each time a search team

reached a new spot, the team leader would report in. But after every search, the news was always the same—no roaches.

"It makes no sense," Jared said. "We're running out of places to look."

"What about the Warm Springs caves?" Jean asked.

"I'd forgotten about those caves," Jared said. "They'd make a perfect nesting place. It's better than any barn or cellar. The caves have everything a roach could want."

Dr. Swanson seemed interested. "What makes those caves so great?"

"They're heated by natural warm springs," Jean said. "Jared and I got to know those caves well when we were kids. I don't think too many people know that much about them."

"The inner chambers are dark, warm, and damp," Jared said. "Those are ideal conditions for roaches to hide and breed." He pointed to a spot in the middle of the map. "Look, the caves are right about here."

"I don't have a search team in that area," the sheriff said worriedly.

"Then let's go! We'll have to check it out ourselves," Jean said.

The drive to the caves seemed to take forever. But Jean knew it was only a ten-minute ride. The sheriff parked close to the entrance. "Does everyone have a flashlight?" he asked.

"We need to be as quiet as we can," Dr. Swanson said. "We don't want to upset the bugs."

"You're not kidding," Jared said sarcastically. "I don't plan to provide another meal for a super roach! Sheriff, what's your idea to get rid of the bugs when we do find them?"

"I have spare cans of gasoline in the trunk," McKay said. "I think we could burn them out."

Just before entering the cave, Jared

turned on his flashlight. The bright beam moved slowly over the walls and ceiling of the cave.

"Nothing," Jean said.

"This is only the first chamber," Jared reminded her. "There are several more chambers just down the tunnel."

The twins headed for the tunnel on the far side of the chamber. McKay followed right behind them. But Dr. Swanson held back. "I am claustrophobic," the scientist said in a shaky voice.

"You're supposed to be the expert. Are you telling me you want to stay here?" Sheriff McKay asked disgustedly.

Dr. Swanson shook his head. His face was red with embarrassment. "No, no, of course not. Let's stay together," he said.

They entered the next chamber. At the center of the cave, warm water bubbled up in a pool. The air was heavy with humidity.

"How much farther do we have to go?"

Dr. Swanson asked nervously. Jean glanced at him. The scientist's face was white with fear. Drops of sweat beaded on his forehead.

Jean was worried. The last thing they needed was to have someone in the group fall apart.

"There's only one more chamber to check," Jared said.

They crept through the opening into the next chamber. Jean suddenly gagged. "Oh, that awful smell!"

Jared nodded and smiled grimly. "I think we've found the nest."

Chapter 9

Jared shone his flashlight beam around the walls of the cave.

Jean gasped. She got out her phone. Unbelievable! It was almost as if the cave itself was alive! The walls and ceiling were plastered with the super bugs. On every surface, dark-winged bodies fluttered, wriggled, and hissed. The floor of the cave was thickly littered with their droppings. And everywhere Jean looked, she saw egg cases. Some were empty. Others were still closed.

Jared and Sheriff McKay splashed gasoline around the room. The bugs immediately seemed to sense that something was wrong. Some of them began to fly about and hiss loudly.

"Okay," Jared said softly. "We've got to hurry and get out of—"

All of a sudden Dr. Swanson screamed. A huge bug had landed on his arm. McKay reached over to pull it off. But the terrified scientist seemed to be going crazy with fear and pain. He pushed the sheriff aside. Then he threw back his head and shrieked.

Swanson's terrified scream startled the roaches. Their ear-piercing hissing now became even louder. Then a dense cloud of super bugs rose into the air. The sound of their beating wings seemed to excite the others.

Jared grabbed Dr. Swanson's arm. He pushed the trembling scientist back into the tunnel. "Go on!" he yelled at Jean and the sheriff.

"What about you?" Jean cried out.

"I have to light the gasoline," Jared answered. "I'll be with you in a minute."

Jean smelled smoke and gas as she took

off running. Then she heard the crackle of flames. She glanced back over her shoulder. Jared was running right behind her, still holding the gas can.

Suddenly the sheriff cried out. Jean turned to look. McKay was trying to shake off several huge roaches that were clinging to his back!

Desperate to help, Jean used her flashlight to brush the bugs off the sheriff's jacket. One of the roaches flew into her face, hissing. Jean screamed as the giant insect dug into her skin. She felt a stab of hot pain as it bit into the soft flesh of her cheek.

She pulled at the roach with all her strength. But when it came away, another took its place. Then someone grabbed her arm. She felt herself being pulled out of the cave.

"Jean!" her brother yelled. He swatted off the roaches. Then he smashed them on the ground.

"I'm okay!" she cried out. "What about the others?"

"We're right here," McKay said. She turned and saw that blood was running down his face. Dr. Swanson looked like he was about to faint.

"We need a first aid kit," Jean said.

"No time!" Jared yelled. "We have to block off the entrance." He grabbed an armful of wood. The others did the same. Soon they had the entrance tightly crammed with kindling. The few roaches that escaped were quickly smashed.

"Good! We can't let any of them get away," Dr. Swanson cried.

Jared set the brush on fire. More bugs were caught in this second blaze. Everyone watched as the roaches burned.

Jean threw more dry brush onto the fire to make sure it wouldn't go out. McKay used his car radio to call the other teams for assistance.

Hours later, Jean sat on a nearby

rock. She watched a team of government scientists enter the cave. It was this team's job to verify that all the roaches were dead. The egg cases had to be destroyed too.

An agent had taken away her phone. He'd promised to return it quickly. She didn't know if what she'd filmed had been any good.

Jared came to sit next to her. "This has been a crazy two days," he said. "I want a normal summer after this."

"Me too," Jean said.

"I heard that we have to sign something," Jared said. "We're not supposed to say what we saw."

"Oh?" Jean said. "Believe me, I don't want to remember it."

"Guess what?" he said, giving her a friendly poke in the arm. "Sheriff McKay just talked to Weaver on the radio. The amusement park opened half an hour ago. It seems to be a great success."

Jean smiled. She was too tired and sore to care very much.

"And here's some news you will care about," Jared went on. "The sheriff told Weaver that he owes us. To show his appreciation, he promised to give us some great-paying jobs this summer!"

By this time, Jean's eyes were sparkling. "Really?"

"Weaver thinks it would be a great idea for you to run one of the new rides. I suggested he assign you to the Centipede!"

Jean's shriek of protest almost drowned out Jared's howl of laughter.

Comprehension Questions

Recall

1. Why did Mr. Wilson have to be taken to the hospital?

2. What was the name of the company that was breeding super roaches?

Who and Where?

1. Who was building an amusement park on the island?

2. Where did the searchers finally find the super roaches?

Vocabulary

1. Jean is most interested in the study of genetics. What does the word *genetics* mean?

2. When he examines a super roach, Jared thinks they have discovered a new species. What does the word *species* mean?

3. Dr. Swanson is claustrophobic. What does the word *claustrophobic* mean?

Cause and Effect

1. What was the cause of Hannah Bowen's visit to the sheriff's office?

2. What was the cause of Jared's belief that Hannah had sold out?